T0103554

Spaces
in
Togetherness

Spaces

in

Togetherness

Bhuban Basu

With a Foreword by
Ramapada Chowdhury

PARTRIDGE
A Penguin Random House Company

Copyright © 1997, 2015 by Bhuban Basu.
First published in Bengali as *Chitraboha* by Shanti Book Stores, Kolkata, 1997

ISBN: Softcover   978-1-4828-4838-0
               eBook   978-1-4828-4837-3

All rights reserved. No part of this book may be used or reproduced by any means, graphic, electronic, or mechanical, including photocopying, recording, taping or by any information storage retrieval system without the written permission of the publisher except in the case of brief quotations embodied in critical articles and reviews.

Because of the dynamic nature of the Internet, any web addresses or links contained in this book may have changed since publication and may no longer be valid. The views expressed in this work are solely those of the author and do not necessarily reflect the views of the publisher, and the publisher hereby disclaims any responsibility for them.

Print information available on the last page.

To order additional copies of this book, contact
Partridge India
000 800 10062 62
orders.india@partridgepublishing.com

www.partridgepublishing.com/india

Contents

To my parents who are not with us today,
My wife, Gayetri,
And daughters, Anindita and Arpita

Foreword

What I felt right at the beginning on reading these stories, is that Bhuban Basu has beautifully captured the essence of that craft called the short story. The stories are quite short, yet within that limit of extent—which is a salient feature of a short story—he has been able to express a clear conclusion beautifully. The faces caught in these stories are not residents of Mars, we see them around us every day. Their dreams, the shattering of those dreams, their aspirations, anxieties, joys and worries are not unknown to us. Within those very human perimeters, he engages the readers in the dilemmas of many unexpected possibilities. And that is when, around those familiar faces, the mystery of the unfamiliar deepens. When a book like this finds appreciation, one must understand that the lay reader is never mistaken in recognizing the real thing even in the midst of a host of fakes.

Calcutta, 1997   Ramapada Chowdhury

A Touch of Feeling

It was just after five. The office was nearly empty save for the two of them. Any other day they would have packed up by now. An important fax message was awaited, the reply to which had to be faxed the same evening.

Somesh sat in his chair rocking mildly. In front of him, at the other side of the table sat Shanta, his secretary. The parting glow of the winter sun had cast a purple spell in the room—lingering, reluctant to leave.

Three years ago Shanta had joined the company as his secretary. She excelled in her work and in no time had established herself as one of the best in the organization. Between the two of them, they had an enviable relationship. Slow process without purpose or intention—mellow, soft and reassuring—entirely official. They were, however, aware of each other's vibes.

As a woman, Shanta had a wholesome appeal. She was graceful, attractive and mature. Intellectual curiosity and social poise made her a cut above others in her profession. She was, however, seemingly vulnerable.

Both of them were relaxed, waiting for the fax message to come through. The faint hum of the homebound traffic from down below was barely audible. Toying with the paperweight on the table, Somesh broke the enveloping silence, "Know something, Shanta? Middle age is a rather difficult period." He paused. "It's . . . it's like going through your adolescence a second time. Only, you are less confident!" Shanta hung on his words for a while, trying to comprehend. Then she retorted, "But aren't you confident?" "Oh!" he smiled, "I don't mean the apparent confidence. What I mean is that you are too aware of the world around you. You are thoroughly corrupted." He lit a cigarette. Latching on to the same thought process he continued, "Yet things happen to you without you realizing them."

"Like what?" she asked innocently. He hesitated. Pondered. Then, without looking up, said, "I am forty-seven. Hair greying all over. A wife at home who cares and a delightful teenaged daughter!" He paused. "Nothing lacking, really," he confided.

She looked at him, mock serious yet receptive. She was all ears. Curious thoughts were trying to crowd her mind. She deliberately tried to avoid them. "Well, to tell you the truth," he continued, "after working with you all these years your face has started distracting me." His sudden frankness both excited and confused her.

She sat in front of him blushing. The mosaic of their fixed relationship was shifting around them, threatening to break their peaceful worlds. She regained her composure soon enough and said in an unhurried way, "I don't know. All I know is I have started liking you more than I should." He kept quiet for some time. Then chose his words carefully. "Probably it is the you I like behind that face." Became thoughtful again and added, "And that is not right, I mean, the way I have started liking you."

Evenings like these come once in a lifetime: to caress, soothe and linger. The memory is almost always sweet but painful. They add meaning to life. Give you time off to dream. So real yet so ethereal. Untouchable. You could only wish circumstances like these would continue.

"I like you too. Working with you has become a habit with me." She heard her words surface slowly, almost surreptitiously. She was both happy and sad at the same time. She was trying to say something more. But you cannot always begin where you leave off.

Suddenly, the telephone began to ring. It was the fax machine. Shanta stood up and the pencil between her fingers came to life again, as it were, and she could almost hear what Somesh would say—"Reference your query of even date . . ."

The Private Truce

An air of expectancy hung about the office. Even a stranger would have sensed it. The monthly board meeting was in progress. Any other time, the board meeting would have been a routine affair. This time, however, it was not. At least, people outside the board room thought so. Two top-level appointments were on the agenda.

The office grapevine was working overtime. The centre of gossip was Kalyan Chaudhury, better known as Colin. It was a foregone conclusion that he would become the Executive Director-Commercial. There was justification for this optimism. He was closest to the kingmaker, Rakesh Tandon, the Managing Director. And what was more important, Colin's wife, Sheila, better known as Sheelu, was even closer.

Scruples were beyond Colin's philosophy of life. He was, as his ever-changing wide circle of friends knew too well, fond of the lighter aspects of living. He was fond of women, fonder of drinks, but his passion was his career. As far as career was concerned, no depth was too low to stoop to. He respected the principal more than the principle.

Cradled in the comforts of a well-heeled existence, Colin had a rather smooth upbringing. Public school education gave him social polish and a management diploma from an obscure university in the States, obtained through sheer perseverance in the face of alluring odds, secured for him the job of a purchase executive in a blue-chip multi-national at a comparatively early age. His family belonged to the commercial aristocracy with strings to pull at the right places and accordingly, his pay packet was from the start higher than most in similar positions.

He had a way with his subordinates, which made him likable without being respected. His flattery of his superiors was effective without being subtle. Colin made it his business to know which way the wind blew. He was always on the right side of things and made friends with a purpose. He was not interested to know who a person was; it was more important for him to know what he was. He worked on the rare talent to endure incompatible company when he knew it would serve his purpose. In short, Colin was destined to reach the top. For him, the end justified the means.

He proved his point. Before reaching the mid-thirties, Colin had acquired a cushy job, a company car and an attractive wife along with a sizeable property thrown in as a bonus, while his friends struggled to keep premature greyness at bay in lesser-known organizations. He was now standing on the threshold of further glory.

Sheila, his wife, was sophisticated, cultured, attractive, articulate and desirable. She was everything that Colin was not. She was altogether better human material than her husband. But Colin's influence was irresistible and the effects were increasingly becoming apparent. All the while, however, though Colin was successful in converting his wife to his way of thinking, the gap in their relationship was widening. Close as they lived physically, emotionally they were drifting apart. Their beautiful house had ceased to be a home. Scenes of growing mutual annoyance were being enacted as a matter of routine.

"Can't you keep your voice low?" she said appealingly. "It's indecent for a gentleman to make so much noise."

"Don't you try to teach me manners, you bitch!"

She frowned. "Funny, of all people you should call me that! I started as a housewife all right. It's you who encouraged me into becoming a . . ."

"Stop it," he blurted. "Wish you had found some other time to pick on me. We are in it together, remember? Whatever you have done, it's for us. Us, do you hear . . . us." His words spilled over each other.

"Us?" she mocked him, lips curling in disdain.

She got up from the table to switch off the boiling kettle and continued the tirade. "Don't kid yourself, Colin. As far as you are concerned it's always been you and only you. I don't even exist when it comes to your career." She was livid. Finally, she snapped with an almost inaudible whisper. "I am just another person you have used."

Suddenly her agony exploded into physical discomfort and she felt too weak to remain standing. She broke down in sobs, uncontrollable sobs.

Colin looked at the clock on the dining room wall. The board meeting was due in an hour. He would have to leave in fifteen minutes.

★

There wasn't much on today's agenda. Other than sanctioning a loan to a sister company in the group, the only important task was the selection of two Executive Directors. The seven directors sat across from each other around the gleaming teak table. Except for Rakesh Tandon, none of the others had any trace of anxiety on their faces. This was to be expected. None of the others were working directors. They weren't really involved in the affairs of the company. One couldn't expect them to be, either. They were at the helm of affairs of so many companies! All of them were directors, as it were, by profession. All they were interested in was their fee. All the work that had to be done had already been done; all the decisions that had to be taken were already taken. Sharpened pencils were lying all but unused. So were the thin bond-paper pads. Rakesh Tandon was completely in charge. All the nods had already been obtained. The meeting was over. They were looking forward to the excellent lunch this company was known to serve. And of course, the large pegs of Gordon's gin, with a dash of lime for some, plain tonic water for others.

Colin waited in his office, perspiring in anticipation. He knew the board meeting was over.

The telephone rang, but later than expected. He could feel that Raghavan, the company secretary and one of his friends, was at the other end of the wire. Seconds of stifled silence prevailed. "Sorry Colin, better luck next time." Colin went speechless—as if stunned by life.

Someone had tread on his dream and the broken pieces of porcelain fantasies lay all around him. He put the receiver down, shocked, incensed and utterly exhausted. For the first time Colin realized that his room did not have any windows and that air-conditioned rooms could be uncomfortably stuffy. His mind lay paralyzed for some time. Inevitably, his fingers dialled his wife's number as his senses started warming up. He knew his wife had picked up the phone. He could say nothing. Neither could she.

Eventually, her name crawled out of his lips.

"Sheelu . . . they . . ."

"I know," she replied with an alien remoteness in her voice. Shocks were hitting Colin like turbulent waves away from the beach. He felt eggshells under his feet, but continued—

"You know? You mean you knew it all along!"

"Yes, for some time now. Ironically, the day I spent with Rakesh."

She waited for him to flare up as usual. The breeze was there, but the flames did not come up this time. He was pleading instead.

"Why? Sheelu why? Why didn't you tell me this before? Don't you have a heart any more?"

His voice almost broke. He was down and under.

Sheila realized that he was in desperate need of warmth and unalloyed affection.

"It's because I have one that I couldn't bring myself to break the news to you." Sheila fell silent. She could visualize the hurt he was nursing and tried to infuse into the words and her voice a new tenderness.

"You know Colin, there's more to life than a promotion." She paused.

She continued with great effort, like a patient in pain.

"If you had succeeded, the success would have been yours. Now that you have failed, the failure is ours." She took her breath, fought desperately to hold back the tears and blurted, "It's funny how people react. After his passion was spent, Rakesh had told me—as if it had nothing to do with me, as if he was speaking of somebody I didn't even know—'Tell me how I can trust a man who has no scruples . . . after all, the company has to come first . . .'"

She was not audible any more, her voice drowned in her sobs. Colin felt her warm tears run down his cheeks.

Are You Listening?

H e asked.

They were both going through their habitual routine of reading in bed before turning in for the night.

She did not reply.

He repeated, a shade louder, "Are you listening?"

She looked at him, rather irritated, and said, "No."

"Oh! I see. You must be reading something interesting then."

"I am," she replied curtly.

Silence prevailed and the reading continued. But the man got impatient.

"It must be one of those damn women's lib articles."

She sat up, looked him straight in the eye and said, "If you must know, the article is all about what the modern man looks for in a woman."

He feigned enthusiasm all over.

"Let's hear some of it," he said. "Must be intriguing?"

"Hardly," she said sarcastically. "Besides, I know what you look for in a woman."

Back to the magazine she went.

He slid back on his pillow and tried to concentrate on reading again.

Bed lights burned. Time was past eleven. The only noise that punctuated the silence was the ruffle of magazine pages occasionally.

He became impatient. Took a chance again. "You know, it's just a thought. Nothing more than an exchange of ideas. I mean, it would be interesting to know . . ."

"I am listening, go on," she said quietly without lifting her eyes.

"Good. How would you feel if I were to tell you that I was having an affair?" he blurted out.

"Having an affair?" she said in a curious voice.

"Yes, an affair." He nodded and looked at her. A faint mischievous smile played on his lips.

"Why do you want to know?" she enquired.

"No reason in particular, you know. People do have affairs, don't they?" He went all coy. "Trying to see your reaction to a hypothetical situation. Sort of psychology test, you may say."

She appeared amused.

"I see," she said thoughtfully.

"Is it because you are interested to know my attitude towards marital fidelity?"

"No," he said, like a quiz master, as if the two were playing a game where more than one answer was allowed.

"Is it that you are about to write the first story of your life or something?" This time there was sarcasm in her voice.

His looks were enough to confirm the negative.

"Perhaps you have the usual itch, you know, men get naughty at. . ." she was almost laughing.

"Ha ha! Nothing of the sort. Try again. I just want to know." He was enjoying the game.

"Are you having an affair?" She became suddenly serious.

"Yes." It came out inadvertently.

The suddenness of the question had forced an immediate response.

"No, what I meant was . . ." he tried to recover, in an attempt to become defensive.

But it was too late.

She shut the magazine, tossed it on the bedside table and sat up.

The game had just begun.

A Change of Heart?

The tea garden lay tucked away in a secluded spot near the foothills of Bhutan. Many years of traffic must have passed through the national highway nearby without noticing it. It is a striking place which would captivate anyone on a maiden visit. The name is Acacia.

Stretching up to the disappearing horizon on all sides, the palette of verdant shades is a feast for the eyes. The vast expanse even threatens to paint the blue of the sky green. Bungalows, like oases, hide behind shade trees great distances apart in the desert green. As you drive along the narrow roads tunnelled by shade trees, girls, young and old, clad in sarees of various hues with cloth bags strapped to their foreheads, pluck tea—heads barely seen above the green growth. In the distance, thick-forested hills rise into low clouds. In the evening, shadows tiptoe down the mountains and silently envelop the surrounding habitat. In the quiet stillness of unrelieved darkness, the drone of insects creates a monotony which irritates the unaccustomed ear.

Amidst these picturesque sylvan surroundings, to the right of the garden office, some distance away, a two-storeyed white bungalow glistens in the sun during the day and the floodlight at night. The red tiled roof and the dark green bushes almost keeping out of view the ground floor

lend the house a charming air. This is the "bara-kothi"—
the manager's bungalow. Tapan and Rina lived here.

Rina had been brought up in an urban atmosphere.
When she was married at the age of 23, her husband was
the deputy manager of Acacia tea garden. Initially, she
wasn't enthusiastic about spending her life away from
the city but was persuaded by her parents into marriage
with Tapan Chowdhuri. Tapan was a handsome man
approaching his thirties, confident in his work and polished
in his social interactions. Soon after Rina arrived in the tea
garden, she took a liking to the place. The cordial reception
she received, the expanse of the unending green and the
hills all around immediately caught her imagination. Her
winsome ways soon made her popular. Her married life
promised both hope and happiness.

*

The garden office was nearly empty. It was late evening.
All his colleagues had left. Pravat had finished the daily
report and was preparing to leave. A message came that
the Barasaab wanted to see him. He felt irritated but did
not show it.

Pravat stood in front of the huge desk. In tea gardens,
usually there are no chairs on the other side of the manager's
table. In keeping with the generally accepted norms,
assistants are not supposed to sit. They stand. Pravat stood
in front of his master like an obedient servant.

Tapan rang the bell and instructed his attendant to bring in a chair. This was most unusual and Pravat was surprised. This hadn't happened before nor was he aware of this happening elsewhere in his few years in the gardens.

"Sit down," said Tapan quietly.

★

For Rina, life in the garden after twelve years of marriage, however, had changed. Tapan had graduated to manager more than seven years ago. The excitement of being the first lady of the garden had collapsed into a predictable routine with the expected adulations. The anxiety and strain of bringing up the two young children had ceased. Her ability to hire and keep competent domestics ensured a smooth and uninvolved household. The mali kept the lawn and the garden trim with flowers bobbing up at the right places in the right seasons. She had all the time in the world to get bored and often ended up doing nothing except wondering how she could keep herself occupied.

Somehow, she remained as attractive as ever. Tallish and lean, she had a well-proportioned body and cascading black hair that she would gather into a neat bun just above her slender nape, taking a few years off her face. Conjugal life, in view of Tapan's increasing involvement in work, brought about by his promotion and the management's dependence on him, had become somewhat stale. Some stimulation outside marriage was felt necessary to rekindle the fire of physical intimacy with her husband, where reciprocation from his side seemed remote.

In this atmosphere, in walked Pravat, a young man in his late twenties. He had been around for a couple of years and, like the rest of them, had shown the respect and reverence due to her. The silver jubilee of the club brought them together as members of a small organizing committee, of which Rina was the chairperson. Frequent meetings, sometimes along with others, and sometimes without, brought them close. Gradually, almost too close for comfort. A malleable character, Pravat was prepossessing and full of the spirit of comity, and ultimately could not resist her deliberate vulnerability. An affair started— initially flimsy, then covertly intimate, culminating in passionate secret sessions.

*

Tapan lifted his eyes, looked at him straight and his voice, without betraying any emotion, slowly rolled out, "I know about you two. You and my wife, I mean."

The suddenness and casual nature of the remark knocked Pravat out. His capacity to realize what was being said snapped. With vague astonishment he could feel his whole being struggling to stay put while his physical self wanted to run as fast as his legs could carry him.

"Mind you," Tapan continued, "I don't blame you, these things are known to happen. Of course, I wish it didn't happen to me."

He casually lit a cigarette.

"I am not quite sure when it started. It has cooled off now, hasn't it? Actually, considerably, if I am not mistaken, since your marriage," Tapan concluded.

★

Long after the jubilee celebrations were over, the assignations had continued. Tapan became vaguely aware of it only after it had become a periodic routine. At first indifferent, he came upon situations which called for dissembling diffidence. He literally lay in wait till he was confident of his wife's infidelity. He was more surprised and hurt than angry. He was, however, too mature to flare up and create a scene. On the contrary, he set upon a self-inquisition. He almost sensed and even firmly believed that all along he had unwittingly contributed to the continuing of the affair. In what way, though, he had yet to find out.

Tapan felt the embers of tension smouldering within himself. He realized, at the same time, that it was a rather delicate situation which called for all his guile if his marriage was to be saved and put back on the rails. And he wanted to save his marriage desperately.

His reasoning bore fruit. He had taken his wife for granted. Their relationship had settled into a loop of absent-minded affection. He had become indifferent to the affairs of his home, while she was losing interest in the official situations. They had stopped reaching for each other. It was time, he thought, to revive his dormant interest in her. He was convinced that their marriage was in need of more emotional investment from his side. As a start, he embarked on a long holiday.

The holiday in Kashmir had a salubrious effect on their marriage. After joining back work, he made it a point to return from office early, played with his kids, visited friends with his wife in the evenings. On occasion, he did not conceal his intention of going to bed early to make love. His rediscovered interest in his family, coupled with the news of Pravat's marriage, lifted his spirits. And by the time Pravat was back in the garden with his wife, Tapan sensed that the old affair had run out of steam. In fact, Pravat had already started to keep away from his wife without making it too apparent. Having thus succeeded in injecting life back into his marriage, Tapan felt confident enough to focus his attention on Pravat.

*

"You love your wife, don't you?" Tapan made a casual enquiry. Pravat didn't know what to reply. Tapan repeated himself. Pravat nodded.

"I thought as much," Tapan mused.

There was a long silence.

"Actually, I think there ought to be some reciprocation," said Tapan and waited.

Again, an uncanny calm prevailed. Pravat, feeling that his boss was waiting for him to speak, said, "I don't understand, sir."

"Well, I think, it's up to you to convince your wife. There's no hurry, you know. Take your time. I will let you know when I am ready."

Pravat sat there, shocked, incensed, petrified. His whole world exploded. The future suddenly disappeared like water down a sinkhole. A few minutes passed without a sound from either side. "That will be all," said Tapan. "Goodnight."

He seemed a different man altogether; a man who concealed his feelings behind a facade of mock indifference. In all these years, Pravat hadn't known that life could be so cruel. He wished he hadn't been born. He felt utterly helpless. The entire conversation left an insipid aftertaste and he cursed himself for his indiscretion. As he recalled his wife's innocent face and the rhapsodic memories of their tender moments together, he felt anxiety rising within him, induced by apprehension and guilt. How do you even broach a subject like that with your wife, leave alone suggest the most distasteful, impossible, outrageous . . . He wasn't able to concentrate on the subject any further. As his Lambretta groaned, he could not, however, help feeling empathy for the man he had just met, actualizing his hurt when he had first found out about them. This somewhat assuaged his helplessness, although it did not relieve him from his fears which had started taking protean forms.

★

The fear of something dreadful happening to their happy married life in the near future adversely affected his conjugal relationship, his enthusiasm for work and life generally. There appeared to be no reprieve from the turmoil that kept raging within him. He kept worrying all the time, lost his ability to concentrate, became distraught and restless. Pravat's wife could guess that something was bothering him but her repeated enquiries fell on deaf ears and no amount of coaxing could milk an answer from him.

For the first time, Pravat painfully realized that love was larger and more demanding than passion. Life changed beyond recognition but had to be lived. He collapsed under the crushing weight of the fearsome tomorrow. Days passed haltingly. Ever since that meeting, Pravat stood shakily on the tightrope of his miserable, lonely self. His premarital misadventure exuded only the faded fragrance of a pressed flower.

Pravat and his wife were sitting in the covered verandah of their bungalow. It was just after dusk. Thick black clouds hung low. Blue streaks of neon flew across the sky in gay abandon. And thunder came in its wake, pounding the earth with irregular frequency. The violent gale threatened to displace everything in its stride. And then it came down with a vengeance. The rain. The wind-swept rain whiplashed the back of the atmosphere like a crazy schoolmaster out to get the truth out of his reluctant pupil. Trees ducked, the scorched earth softened its rough tones and hell broke loose on earth. The first signs of a nor'wester, Pravat thought.

It subsided in half an hour. The evening became cool, pleasant. The only trace of rain and wind was left in the reflection of the shining bulbs in the puddles and the scattered leaves lying all round.

The telephone tinkled in the bedroom. Pravat got up to answer it.

"Hello," he said.

"Good evening, Pravat. Chowdhuri here. Could you two come over now? It's a delightful evening."

Pravat heard the sound of the receiver being placed back on the holder. A chill ran down his spine. He felt weak in the knees. He knew Rina was away with the kids for a few days and Tapan was alone. The moment had arrived.

★

When the two arrived in the manager's bungalow, Tapan was in his dressing gown, smoking a pipe. Uneasily, Pravat sat down.

"The rain is most welcome. The heat was becoming oppressive lately," said Tapan. Pravat listened, confused. While he sat now knowing what was expected of him, Tapan and his wife indulged in irrelevant talk that usually follows such meetings.

"Oh! By the way, Pravat," Tapan interjected suddenly, "Have you finished making all the arrangements for the monthly dinner day after tomorrow?"

"Well, in fact, sir, I am supposed to be going down to the club," Pravat got up.

"Yes, I think you should. You run along and come back here as soon as you finish." Tapan almost pushed him down the stairs with his words.

Pravat's wife sat still, oblivious of the entire situation. As Pravat's two-wheeler coughed to a start, Tapan suddenly rushed from his seat and down the stairs and called out to Pravat. He slowly went over to him, put his right hand on his shoulder and, while the engine still droned, said to him in a very soft voice, "Relax, you have sweated out enough heat, I imagine, in the last few months, haven't you?"

"Sir!" a surprised Pravat exclaimed.

"You have, I know what it's like. I only wanted you to feel some of the anguish I went through. It's hell," Tapan said almost philosophically. "I don't mean any harm. Let's all go to the club and have a drink."

He turned around and ran up the stairs while Pravat stood speechless. As he stopped the engine of the scooter, he could hear Tapan's jovial voice ring out like a bell. He was addressing Pravat's wife, "Come on, let's all go down to the club for a drink and celebrate the first rain of the season."

Crisis of Confidence

I wished the night could begin all over again. Dawn was breaking through the film of gradually disappearing darkness. The lawn-grass lay bathed in morning dew. An autumn breeze gently blew carrying the hint of winter chill. Flowers still drooped with lingering laziness. The two of us stood on the lawn, tired after the nightlong revelry, whispered intimacies and little pleasures. Sushmita looked up at me. Melting eyes craving, pregnant with purpose. Gratitude written all over her face. I took her hand, looked into her eyes and perspired. I wished the night could begin all over again but . . .

This was the first time our families were meeting after nearly two years. Last evening was similar to the one two years ago, on the eve of our departure to Singapore. During the intervening period, letters were written, greeting cards exchanged. Hopes were expressed on both the families coming together again, like old times. Last evening had been that evening. Our first meeting in nearly two years. My impression was that their lives had become rich in family pleasures. She was beaming. Sushmita's husband was buzzing about her like a bee. Yet, I wanted to hear it from her. Hear that she was happy. That life for them wasn't any more a jog-trot of indifferent affection. I felt the crushing weight of conscience lift. It was like being told by the doctor that the ECG was clear and there was nothing to worry about.

"You look good," I said. "Hope you feel that way too."

"Yes," she whispered, "and thank you very much."

"Don't thank me, thank yourself. It's you who made it possible."

"True," she retorted, "but you showed me the way. You didn't know how I would react, did you? You were taking a hell of a chance, weren't you?"

"Perhaps," I said.

I came to know Sushmita through Alka, my wife. She was my wife's colleague at the nursery where they both taught. Intimacy didn't take long to develop between the two families. In the claustrophobic atmosphere of the small town, their company opened windows for fresh draughts. Our children became very friendly with their daughter. In no time, both the families became inseparable. But familiarity didn't breed contempt; instead, it made us discover the skeletons in each other's cupboards.

"Yes, it all began so suddenly . . . Funny after all these years. None of us even thought about it."

"I remember it vividly . . . can't think of it. You know . . . this happening again with someone else," I said, "I am to blame perhaps . . ."

"And my protest was too feeble . . . Perhaps I craved for someone to reach me, you know . . . Not just touch . . . Well, that I was getting all the time, wasn't I?" she laughed.

We both laughed.

The recipe for happiness is illusory, almost like orgasm. One may suddenly get a firm hold of it and not know how to repeat the performance. Happiness had eluded the couple often. Ajay thought he knew what he wanted from her, knowing she could not give it to him. Sushmita thought she had given all a man could want and knew not what else a woman could give.

"We have turned over a new leaf," she said, drawing me closer as the theme from *Elvira Madigan* filled the air with its magical rhythm.

"I am glad, really glad!" I meant it.

"I shall always remain grateful. You know that, don't you?"

"You needn't, you know! While trying to make you discover yourself, I have discovered myself, so to speak." I told her.

"Oh! How is that?" she enquired.

"I am not quite sure, you see. Just a thought. Am I a hypocrite? I mean, it's true I wanted to see you happy, but was that an excuse to come closer to you?"

"Never thought that way! Although I must admit, I did feel guilty at times. After all, I am a married woman." She paused. "Maybe I longed for company, you know, sympathy and all that. Our marriage was literally on the rocks, you know that."

There was silence for some time. Then she spoke again. "But why did you have to wait till the very last day? We had known each other for four years. You had never even made a pass at me."

"That's the only reason my conscience brings up every time I feel shaky. After all, I am a happily married man. I can't afford to indulge in niceties like this every time I feel like it," I said.

It was a paradox. Two normal people, kind-hearted, helpful and perfect darlings with everyone they came in contact with. Yet, unable to churn out a homespun philosophy to live happily together. Their life could not grow together; sex was the limiting factor. She thought sex to him was like candy, the more, the sweeter. He thought her idea of sex was that although necessary, it was not fundamental to happiness. To him she was frigid; to her, he was over-sexed.

For them, no tomorrow was a vision of hope. The days used to end without purpose, in total disarray. Disappointments and frustrations chased each other to the summits of tolerance and exploded in shouting bursts of acute physical and mental pain. This was the climax of their living together. It was painful to see their seven-year-old daughter, bewildered and agape, waiting for the nightmare to pass.

"Hypocrisy apart, I wonder what is good for society. To live within moral bounds and be unhappy or break a rule or two and find happiness," I mused. "The danger is, of course, that in the process, you may threaten to upset the arrangements of society."

"It is curious, you know. For the first time, I realized that it's difficult to bear happiness alone. You need someone to share it with. Glad you are here."

I was convinced that she was happy. They were a happy family, leading a life to which they were entitled years ago. Better late than never, I thought.

"Our relationship has become normal. At least what I think is normal. We both feel it," she said, sipping from a glass of chilled pineapple juice.

"Didn't he wonder how all this happened? How you changed?" I enquired.

"It didn't happen in a day. As you wanted me to, I became an eager beaver. Gradually made him feel that I enjoyed sex for a change. At times I even made the first move and that surprised him no end. In a way, it was silly," she sounded edgy.

"It paid rich dividends though," I said.

We had chatted incessantly throughout the night. And as dawn broke Sush and I had developed a relationship that had, I thought, surprised us both. We were caught up in a whirlpool of intimacy hitherto unknown and unrecognized. It just happened.

"Thank God we weren't alone that evening . . . anything might have happened . . ."

We were just sauntering up to the lawn. She fell silent. Then she spoke in a hushed voice bordering on the inaudible.

"It still might . . ."

I heard her voice echo my thoughts. That startled me. It was bad enough as it was. No need for a matchstick, eager as I was to be struck like the face of a matchbox. Fighting against myself to keep my desire at bay. Unplanned but inescapable, the touch, the smell and the passion was now threatening to transform a purpose into an affair. My purpose had been served. Our relationship—the twilight one—was over and done with. Prolong it, I thought, and it would spoil the very purpose it was meant to serve.

Dawn was breaking . . . the lawn-grass lay bathed in morning dew . . . the air full of birdsong . . .

I wished the night could begin all over again, but I dared not face it. The delicious time that had passed had to be sentenced to oblivion. Once and for all. I took her hand, looked into her eyes and perspired. Silence became threatening. "Sush," I began, "we shall have to face facts. Come down to earth, you know. You will understand . . . I am sure. In fact, there isn't an alternative."

There was a pause. Then I blurted out.

"From this moment you are Mrs Anand again. My wife's friend . . . my friend's wife . . . you realize don't you . . . thus far and no further . . . that way we stay friends." The speech had been made. I felt relieved. To dilute the atmosphere I added . . .

"Now run along like a good hostess . . . I need breakfast badly . . . I am stark raving hungry."

Love a Little Less, but Longer

Our marriage had become too barren to spring surprises. Somehow, after nearly fourteen years, it was gradually becoming difficult to understand each other. The togetherness was wilting. Even in privacy we became almost strangers.

My wife was feverishly occupied in discharging her duties as a mother and a housewife. In the daytime, when she was not busy in the kitchen, she was either dropping off or picking up our daughters from school. She faithfully devoted all her evenings to ensure that the homework of the children was complete. The house was being given the usual rubdown. I got my breakfast and dinner on time, hot and palatable. We hardly conversed during the day, except for exchanging absolute necessities. At night, when we went to bed, she was asleep before I could so much as say hello. Hers was a brilliant performance for onlookers, but to me, it was intensely irritating. She was, I felt, ignoring me.

During this period, work pressure was keeping me in office for longer hours than usual. Sometimes, I brought work home. Late nights, on these occasions, became inevitable. I must admit, I was unable to take part in family life the way a good husband should.

We were both living a life together, alone. After years of happiness, I don't think either of us knew how this situation developed. Maybe we had it too good for too long. We were completely out of the social circuit except to keep appointments which demanded our presence as a matter of courtesy. Literally, we attended weddings and funerals. Outdoors, we maintained a respectable existence—the facade of a happy conjugal life. I am sure a few couples even envied us. We both, however, remained unhappy in an otherwise comfortable life.

To make matters worse, I caught the seven-year itch after fourteen years. Within a month, I took three attractive ladies out, one at a time, to dinner. I had known all of them in the past. To be honest, I enjoyed the evenings. All of them were seeped in urban culture and had enough brains to carry on an interesting conversation. At the same time, they were charming enough to embrace my awareness with thoughts of what might have been. My wife knew all of them, and I told her about my rendezvous. She feigned indifference. Or so I thought, anyway. But instead of being in good humour, with my return home on each occasion, my mood changed. I became irritable.

It was the same home, yet it was another home. I still loved her but was no longer in love with her. She got irritated if I invited friends home. When we were invited, she found excuses to stay behind. What used to be discussions, became shouting matches. Tender moments! Well, I lived through the pages of fiction as a tolerable substitute. We had just stopped listening to each other.

Frankly, the situation at home had me worried to the bone. I believe she too was passing through the same anguish. I searched for a way to reach her, to fall in love with her all over again.

That evening went by like any other. When I went into the bedroom, I noticed a card lying on my pillow. It read:

Dear Hubby,

> *Together, we will be fifteen years old tomorrow. May I have the pleasure of your company tomorrow evening for an informal dinner at our residence at 7 p.m. I have invited some mutual friends. May I solicit your undivided attention and presence in this family reunion.*

Your "once" loving
Now Lonely Wife

I was touched. Like old times, I thought. My eyes stayed dry, but it had started raining inside. For the last couple of years we hadn't celebrated our anniversary.

It had just come and gone with a mutual exchange of presents. The presents had all the glitter that our budgets could afford but the thought behind the gifts was sans imagination.

This was, I thought, a definite move on her part to forgive and forget. I was eager to reciprocate. As soon as she came into the room, I said, "Thank you. It's a pleasant surprise after a long time. What can I do in return?"

"Nothing," she smiled, "just be there." Her smile had sunbeams.

"I will be present, dear, but I meant . . ."

I couldn't finish.

"I didn't mean your physical presence. I mean 'be' there, you know," she squeezed the word to wring the essence out.

"Tell you what? I won't be going to office tomorrow. I'll ring them up in the morning," said I with a great deal of enthusiasm.

She was a breath away from me. "Promise?" she said.

"Promise," I echoed, "and . . . and . . ."

Her lips were in the way.

Snowflakes Disappear Softly

The ingredients of this story are simple. It tells you about the age-old feeling of mutual liking. A liking, which, if given indulgence, has the power to wreak havoc. It is a simple story of a man and a woman. It's not a triangle, although there is a third dimension to it. It is in the form of a woman.

Another woman, the man's wife.

Now let me tell you how this other woman came into our lives. And would you believe it? It's my wife who brought her in. Well, to tell you the truth, unwittingly, of course. It was she who found her out and engaged her to teach our elder daughter. Our daughter was just ten years old. We have two daughters. It was getting rather difficult for my wife to teach both of them. I suggested that we should engage a teacher for the elder one, while she could continue with the younger one who had just turned six.

My wife announced one day that someone would be coming from the first of next month. She is known to a friend of her friend. She is supposed to be very good. Her friend has told her that her daughter has improved since this lady started teaching her. Actually, she is not the professional type, you know. She isn't doing it for money. She is the only daughter of a rather well-to-do retired father.

She teaches because she has a lot of time on her hands. I understand she also works for a firm as their publicity officer. Good student, I believe and rather attractive. My wife was describing her credentials.

"Sounds interesting. Quite a lady, I say. And a spinster? Why, I wonder!" I said half smiling.

"You can ask her yourself." She ignored me.

God! Did I know then that I would be asking that lady the same question myself a few months later. Anyway, more of that later.

The first of the month arrived. And although my wife had told me about her the previous night, when I arrived from office that evening, even the excitement of my daughter wasn't enough to remind me of the guest we were expecting. The doorbell rang. I opened it. A lady was waiting.

"Yes?" I enquired.

"I am Monica Masani. Good evening."

The penny dropped instantly. That's the name my wife had told me.

"Good evening," I said apologetically. "Do come in. My daughter is eagerly waiting for you."

I ushered her into our drawing room.

"I am her father."

"I know."

"You do?" I must have looked surprised. "How?" It came out automatically.

"Well, I have met your wife twice before. I think it was last Sunday. I saw you with your wife at AC Market. Seeing you here today . . ."

"I see. You should have come up then."

"Two of you were busy with your purchases . . ."

My daughter floated into the room. "Hello Aunty." Then in came my wife.

"Right, see you later." I took my leave and left the room.

When my wife came out, I kept smiling.

"What's the matter with you?"

"Nothing!" I said. "Only wished I had a teacher like that. Even at this age."

"You would, wouldn't you," she said in mock anger. "I wonder how long she's going to continue, with you hanging around."

"Thanks for being polite. I almost thought you would be using Lawrence's phrase, 'sniffing around'."

"Don't be vulgar," she scolded me.

I changed the subject. But that lovely teacher's thought lingered in my mind.

So this is how it all began. You must be thinking, so what? Nothing unusual. Yes, indeed! But then, the trouble is, it didn't stay that way. It was just a ripple in the beginning and, like a ripple, didn't freeze. It went on growing—circle after circle. Only, unlike it, it refused to wither. But I tarry—I will tell you how it happened.

She comes three evenings a week. I have got the days by heart. Monday, Wednesday and Friday. Oh! I can see you are making assumptions. No, actually, I didn't see her every evening. Only now and then. But I must be honest. I did make excuses at times to walk into my daughter's room, while she was there. Not regularly, but sometimes. My wife, in the meantime, had become a good friend of hers. I understand she is a couple of years her junior. Apparently the two got on fine. And long after my daughter's coaching would be over, the two of them would sit and chat. They were birds of the same feather, I suppose.

"She is delightful company," my wife confided. "And so are her parents."

"Parents?"

"Yesterday I had been to her house for tea."

"I thought she was a working woman."

"Actually, she's taken a week's leave. Got some work at home."

"What about me?" I said, "I would have loved to come."

"Wouldn't you! But then you weren't invited, were you?"

"I blame you for that. You should have accepted high tea."

"I wish I was a bit like her. Look how independent she is. She runs her own life."

"Oh! Don't I wish that," I said mischievously.

She gave me a glare.

Months passed. Nothing of note happened, except that without realizing it, I had grown fond of her. Although an outsider, she became very much a part of our family routine. My daughters were enamoured of her. My wife became her friend. I was the one who was left out in the cold. Oh! How I wish I had a little bit of her warmth. One thing had, however, started happening to me in her presence. I had started feeling uneasy. She gave off waves, which threatened to throw me off balance.

Things came to a head during my daughter's birthday party. My daughters invited a few of their friends. And, of course, the chief guest was Aunty Monica. I had taken the day off from my usual delicious do-nothing leisure hours as my wife was insistent that I should do my share of duty as well. I was, to say the least, delighted to do so, as I had prior information that Aunty Monica would be there from the afternoon, organizing party games for the children.

Sunday it wasn't. But it was in spirit. For me, it turned out to be a day which would haunt my senses for God knows how long. She arrived in an off-white silk sari with a saffron border—simple, elegant, beautiful. To tell you the truth, she bowled me over. You wouldn't believe it, but I relived, for the first time since I was a teenager, the pangs of love—to hold, be held and belong. It was a delightful feeling but at the same time, painful. I felt ashamed. Ashamed of being able to shed off twenty years, the greyish maturity, of feeling elated at the sight of a woman. But at times, faces can be sheer magic. Her olive-black melting eyes were like windows through which you could see her soul. We exchanged glances—you are bound to—and held each other's eye.

The air, during those few moments, became charged with sensuality. You could almost touch it. Silly man! you must be muttering under your breath. Wait, I say, till it happens to you!

Anyway, while my wife was busy preparing the cheese straws and apple tarts, mutton chops and muffins, I was helping Aunty Monica with her party games. Sometimes I applied glue on small bits of paper, sometimes I put numbers on others—and all the time, both my daughters were fussing over her, bending over backwards to be of help. In between work and rest we talked, exchanged views, kept quiet and laughed. Talked nonsense, all of which sounded at the time full of sense.

It usually does.

"I must thank you for being here with us today," said I.

"I am enjoying it. Thanks for your help."

"It seems you enjoy being with kids."

"Very much," she smiled.

My children came in, spilled a glass of water and messed up the carpet.

"Wonder why you are still alone?"

"Perhaps because I didn't find anyone like you."

"You can't mean it . . ."

"Why not?"

"I am a married man. There's no future for you."

"So what? I can still love you, can't I?"

"What will you gain out of it?"

". . . Gain? Does everything have to have an end? Isn't the journey as enjoyable as reaching the destination?"

Daydreams, like snowflakes, disappear softly . . .

Oh! How I wish you could talk the way you feel. But you can't, you see! Civilized people have to behave in a civilized manner in society. If you are married, you don't express your feelings about other women. It's just not done. And so I didn't express anything to anyone. Well, so I thought, let's say. But then you say you can't stop your eyes from expressing. It gives you away. And it did me. Guess to whom? My wife, of course, who else?

The same evening, the evening we celebrated our daughter's birthday—after the chaotic hurricane had subsided, and the daughters were tucked into bed securely—my wife and I faced each other to take stock of the events of the day.

"Thank you for helping out. Most unlike you, I thought." She was undoing her hair.

"Thanks. Actually my efforts surprised myself."

"Wonder why?"

If you are guilty, you can't feign innocence. I didn't reply.

"I think you should take care. Might burn yourself."

"I believe it's possible. She is capable of sparks. But believe me, I can't help myself." I was serious.

"Should be ashamed of yourself. You are being unfair to Monica."

"What do you mean, unfair?" I objected.

"You know she is vulnerable. She's got to be. And all you are doing is taking advantage of the situation." She wasn't really annoyed. Just concerned.

"What do I do then?" I implored.

"I am sure you're clever enough to find a solution."

That was that. She didn't mention her any more.

Monica will be coming tomorrow evening, as usual. And along with her, will walk in charm, smiles, glances and daydreams.

Tell me, honestly, dear reader, what would you have done?

The Colour of the Rainbow

Yesterday, I came upon a piece of paper. I was rummaging through old papers collected through the years to remind me of days gone by and stumbled upon a pearl. For me, it opened a window through which I gazed at my youth in wonder and awe.

"Open it when you are airborne," she had said and given me an envelope.

"I'll open it before take-off," I had replied.

This is what she had written.

"If ever you become a writer, among your many characters, reserve a small place for me. I know I can't take up much space anyway for there's nothing much to write about. Still, spare a few lines for me. I confide that my feelings for you sit like a cherry on top of everything in my heart. I do hope you will write about me, if at all you write about anybody and I will ring in your writings very softly indeed; it will be as soft as the impression I have made on you, if any at all."

She had given it to me at the airport nearly twenty-five years ago on the eve of my departure to England.

As I pondered over the words etched out superbly on the piece of paper, they leapt up and sat by my ears to sing a song which had once been sung over and over again.

The melody which had drowned in the din of mundane daily living came back and, with it, came the nostalgic affection of a relationship. My thoughts were enmeshed in a personal reverie.

I met Keya when we were both twenty. She was one of those who stood out in a crowd. And she was more than a face. On the contrary, I was one who easily got lost in a crowd. Ironically, however, we felt mutual attraction almost from the time we set eyes on each other. She walked into my life like a dream, like the fragrance of a bunch of roses freshly plucked. A glitter of a liaison developed between us—a mutual vibration of liking, caring and sharing. It was neither infatuation nor love, neither friendship nor passion. It was none, it was all.

She was a livewire, full of joie de vivre. Never moody, depressed or bored, she enjoyed everything she did, always committed to having a wonderful time. Her emotional responses were contagious. She made me happy and motivated within me a drive to explore the possibilities of life. Her boisterous beckoning behaviour had an aura of innocence around it which made her irresistible. She sparkled with charm and wit and dazzled me. I, on the other hand, as she frequently reminded me, enthralled her. Actually, we both luxuriated in each other's company. Both of us were two ordinary human beings—a boy and a girl who had just stepped out of their teens—like many others elsewhere, everywhere. The beauty of it was that we were both convinced that the other one was extraordinary. And we didn't allow a third person to enter our world.

Yet, both of us individually were involved with a third person; I more than her. While I was infatuated with another girl of my age whom I had met a few months before I came to know Keya, she was being wooed by a gentleman, who I take it, was enamoured of her, if not in love with her. However, their affair was passing through a lean stage at that point of time. Be that as it may, nothing happened to disturb the relationship between me and Keya.

None who knew us, however, believed that we were not in love. Some became positively envious. They believed that something must be going on between us. Yet we never even held hands. We were physically detached, yes. But emotionally, well, there we were thoroughly entwined. Before we knew each other, neither of us had ever thought that a relationship like ours was possible. Yet we were living it. And our relationship! There was nothing apologetic about it—no secrecy disguised as innocence. It was as faithful and sincere as a photograph taken by an amateur who was not aware of the techniques of special effects. For both of us, it was the most exciting thing to ever have happened. And we fell in love with life individually and together.

As I handled the piece of paper fondly, memories surfaced and refused to stay submerged, like cork.

One day, while the rest of the class was being bored by dry lectures, we got away from the city to a lovely spot by the river Ganges and were having a wonderful time.

"I wonder how it feels to be in love."

"Are you?" Her eyebrows made a perfect arch.

"Am I what?" I enquired.

"In love!"

"Well," I smiled, "the answer is yes and no."

"That's better," she giggled, "as long as there's a doubt, we are okay."

We both burst out laughing.

"Seriously, I think," she began, "being in love must be a wonderful experience but marriage, well, I don't know, maybe people don't remain the same!"

I was listening. She continued. "It's the habit, you know, of being together all the time, that spoils it, I suppose."

"Maybe," I mildly protested, "we shall both know more about it when we get married."

"Hope that's sometime away," she said with a smile.

"Remind me twenty years from now. I promise to be truthful in my answer."

"We shall see when the time comes," she said thoughtfully.

Our holiday to forever, however, ended rather abruptly. Within a month, I was to leave for England for continuing my studies. The whole month, days became very short and nights too long for us. We spent as much time together as possible. And for an inordinately long time, our telephones remained engaged in the late evenings much to the irritation of our parents. Like all good things, the month slipped away unnoticed, like water on a swan's back. And I left with the promise that I would write to her as often as I could with a minimum of one letter—a long one—a week. She promised me likewise. She also said that hers would be the first letter I would receive abroad.

Sure enough, she kept her promise. She wrote to me at midnight on the evening I left. The first lines of that letter still ring in my ears. Wish I could seal myself inside the envelope. How lucky these papers are! Only she could have expressed herself in this way.

Thus started another chapter. We exchanged letters faithfully, once a week. They became mere extensions of our prolonged conversations. "Your letters bring a breath of fresh air into my routine of stuffy classrooms and not too exacting leisure hours, it affords me an opportunity to dream. I gulp the words down like a thirsty traveller does a glass of cold water on a summer afternoon."

The grey of London and my unrelieved loneliness were only brightened by my anticipation of the arrival of her letters. And each letter arrived like a new bride, waiting for the veil to be lifted! They came unfailingly, once a week. They were affectionate and full of tenderness, encouraging and inspired confidence. They reminded me of the sweet yesterdays and made my todays for sure—all of them exuded the smell of fresh earth and the perfume of sincerity. Each letter reminded me of a line I had read somewhere—as long as there are postmen, life will have zest.

Then there was no letter one week. I wrote as usual. It didn't bother me too much. It was bound to arrive any day. A letter ultimately arrived after two full weeks. The envelope was heavier than usual. I thought she was making up for missing the last week's ration. It was, however, more than I had bargained for. "I am missing you more than I have at any time before. I wish you were here. The gentleman of whom you know and of whom I have been writing to you lately, has proposed to me. He has asked my parents for my hand in marriage, provided, of course, I consent. I have not been able to make up my mind. I have asked for time. He is a sweet person and someone of whom I know a great deal. Let's put it this way—he's no stranger. Please don't answer me in haste. I have all the time in the world. So please, I beg you, take your own time. I am in no hurry. I am prepared to wait. But be honest. I will be waiting for your reply—with bated breath, panting, in anticipation and in hope, in apprehension and I know not what! Do write."

I slept over it for three full days. Read and re-read her letter over and over again. I read the lines, in between the lines, dwelt upon words and phrases to wring out the meaning. Tried to creep inside her head stealthily. And I recalled an exchange of views in our letters where we had both tried to define our exact relationship. She had written, "My love for you is like hope which cannot be satiated, like thirst which cannot be quenched, like a destination which cannot be reached."

"The colour," I had replied, "of our love is the colour of the rainbow." I realized that the time had come to make a black-and-white decision. Having made up my mind, I sat down to reply to her letter.

I woke up from my reverie. As I looked down at the piece of paper in my hand lovingly, I felt satisfied. I had not let her down.

And this is her story. I did keep her word, and my promise—the promise I had made to myself silently as the aircraft was airborne twenty-five years ago, on a cold winter evening over the city of Calcutta—with a little piece of paper fondly held between my fingers.

The Interlude

"**W**ell, I suppose you don't love me any more."

"Oh, I don't know. You can't stop loving someone overnight," she paused. "Not me. Not after all these years, anyway."

The reply had surprisingly reassured him somewhat.

"But of course," she exclaimed, casually combing her cascade of black hair, "I don't trust you any more."

That was it, he thought. That was the end of their togetherness, their rapport.

Like all marriages, it had its ups and downs, even periods of disenchantment, but had always held together. Since that fateful day, however, life for them had changed face beyond recognition. Their home had overnight turned into a house where two adults lived. They slept separately. For the outside world, they maintained a facade of happy living by putting up social appearances wherever necessary and greeting visitors with a warm smile. As far as others were concerned, nothing had changed, but to them, happiness stayed locked up in memory.

Amit knew his wife too well not to realize what he had let himself into. His sudden surge of passion had morally upset her and hurt her feelings. Ratna was a woman of medium build, not particularly attractive, but could make herself appealing if she wished. She was a rather plain girl who looked at life subjectively. To her, life was like an attractively bound book to be left on the shelf for display rather than reading. Sophistication she did not have but carried about her a quiet grace that lent her a personality all her own. She was not open to argument and logic was not something she understood well. Once she made up her mind, she stuck to it. No amount of pleading or reasoning could change her attitude or opinion. Since marriage, she had the upper hand in the affairs of the home which she regarded as her sanctuary. He knew that he had violated the sanctity of this sanctuary which had been so precious to her.

He had resolved to wait till he could convince her by his actions that this would not happen again. Amit felt repentant and swallowed in self-pity realizing that his passions had gone beyond his control. He once again reversed the spool of his thoughts. Nothing had been contrived and yet the incident was serious enough to pull his family life apart. And how he had treasured it all these years!

The damn dance, he thought. He had never been a lover of parties. And yet he had been. Why did he have to go? He had thought about it then too. His wife had gone to see her mother who had been ill for some time. She was gone for nearly two weeks and he was just beginning to feel a shade lonely. So he had decided to attend the Easter dance at the office.

His loneliness, coupled with the absence of any possible explanation, made him lose count of his drinks in no time. The band was good and the lights were dim. It suddenly dawned on him that he had had a fair number of dances with Sandra. With drinks in his head and Sandra's warm body pressing against his, he felt the weight of responsibility hanging low and the immediate factual existence gradually melting into thin air. He began to think there was something in the way she moved that was rather appealing to his senses. He pulled her a little closer. He thought of her shapely legs, her firm round breasts and her inviting lips. The drinks had already diluted his moral Inhibitions, so there was not much resistance from within.

He took his lips close to her ears and whispered, "You dance like an angel." She did not reply. She didn't have to. She just snuggled closer. It was one of those evenings when she breathed only to obey. The clock had by then ticked itself away from midnight. He whispered again, "How about a quiet cup of coffee in my flat? It's rather stuffy in here." "I don't mind," she had mumbled.

She couldn't have said anything else at that time. Off they went to his flat and coffee was hardly the drink that would quench their thirst. Drinks, music, dim lights and the surging passion had transported them to a world where rationality and good sense were creeping out fast.

That Sunday morning had been harrowing for Ratna. She had returned unexpectedly, with a glint in her eye, expecting to see a surprised but happy husband. Amit answered the doorbell. Despite the hangover he was shaken to consciousness as he saw his wife standing at the door. He made a desperate effort to look happy and said, "Oh, but I thought you would let me know. I would have come to the station."

"Mother is well and here I am. A pleasant surprise is better than a fulfilled hope." She almost danced in. Then she looked at him and said, "You don't look happy. What's up?"

Before Amit could answer, she had pushed open the bedroom door. And there she was, lying in bed, still asleep. A gamut of emotions swept through her system—stupefaction, disbelief, exasperation and ultimately sheer cold rage. She stared at him in disgust. Amit's words, usually well punctuated, spilled over each other. "I had been to the Easter dance, you know, and I mean she shouldn't have come, but of course you realize it was late and she couldn't go home at that time of the night. It is useless I suppose to try to explain but believe me it wasn't arranged. It just happened. You have to believe me, darling, please . . ."

On and on he went, round and round, trying to explain, to plead his way out of the rut he had fallen into, realizing that the walls of escape were too high for him to scale. And as he spoke, he heard his disjointed sentences with a sense of utter hopelessness. She merely gazed, shocked and reticent, closed the door, went into the hall and said in a voice muffled with disdain, "Please, I beg you, please ask her to leave at once."

Since then, life for them had stumbled along for nearly three years. Three long years in which smiles had been forced and holidays spent in the lonely company of each other. And each time Amit had tried to bring up the ugly topic, she had snapped the threads ruthlessly: "Darling, please, it makes me sick. Please don't." All his efforts at reconciliation were floored even before they could stand. He had pleaded with her with waning hope but she had refused to give an inch. She was too firm a woman to give up so easily a stand which had been taken after careful deliberation. And at these moments Amit felt that the eternal boy within him was struggling through thirty-five years of manhood.

Ratna's frustration and agony had in no way been less penetrating. She was quite often surprised to find her physical self so anxious for a happy reunion. Her instinctive longing to become a mother debated furiously with her stubborn attitude. And there had been moments when she had felt like making up, to forgive and forget, fling herself into his arms and aspire to the rainbow through her tears. But then the memory of that awful morning would come back in a flash and, with it, would come the shame and indelicacy of it all, to take the wind out of her sails.

Then one day it happened. Happened suddenly, in the afternoon, during her siesta. It was a happy feeling. Her body quivered at the thought of impending pleasure. The apparition closed in on her with outstretched hands, warm and inviting. That embrace she would love to be locked in. His hands were all over her body, exploring and caressing. His lips came down almost touching hers as she felt herself let go. The touch made her start. She sat up. It was just half past four. The apparition, like an imprint on a negative, was almost recognizable but not quite. Her siesta had come to an end but its memory lingered and disturbed her. It was all so misty that her recollections eluded apprehension. She tried hard to pick every loose ribbon of recollection and bind them together towards a common end. She wanted to find out who the apparition was. Then it dawned that he was someone she had met a few days back. A sense of shame washed over her in little waves, obliterating all the satisfaction of physical intimacy like footprints on sand.

She wished she could hide from herself. The feeling of sexual fulfilment she encountered in her dreams appeared only to satisfy the urgency of her physical desires. The feeling somehow made her anticipate the future with optimism but as the refrain of the dreamy satisfaction began to wane, much of that confidence was ebbing, drained by worries that appeared to stretch ahead indefinitely. The new wave of thought rolled on to wet new grounds in her consciousness. And with it, a sense of guilt crept in.

She had a husband whom she loved and still cared for and yet was enjoying the embraces of someone else. She had become unfaithful only in spirit and suddenly realized that it was the same reason that she had pushed her husband away. The sense of guilt held sway and she thought they were both guilty, not in degree perhaps, but in kind certainly. Her flesh had remained true but the spirit had faltered. The way she had deprived her husband and herself seemed unjustified. Had she left her husband, then the pangs of separation would not be greater than it had been all these years; staying together yet living alone.

As these thoughts kept flying around in her head, her longing for him returned with a thud. She was apprehensive about the way reconciliation might be achieved. Amit had made many endeavours in these intervening years to make up, but she had resisted. And yet now she was the one who was ready to forgive and forget so that they could relive the happy days of the past. But what would she say? How would she start a conversation? Suddenly the solitude within her began to ache; to touch the tenderness of another being so close, to love and be loved. And with it gushed forth her instinctive longing for motherhood. She could think no more and began to throb with excitement at the thought of his returning home from office.

When Amit returned home from office that evening, she tried to keep calm and behave normally. But Amit noticed, as the evening matured, with hope trickling through his veins, that her affection was being lavished on him in abundance. Her excitement had begun to filter through. After dinner he smoked his cigarette as usual and as he was getting ready for bed, he noticed her. His wife was standing on the threshold of his bedroom with a pillow in hand. Her lips didn't move but her eyes, moist with tears of repentance, were shouting forgiveness in loud bursts. Amit got up from the bed, speechless. His lips twitched and a faint smile played on them. Ratna stood there waiting, hearing her heart pounding within. The silence between them trembled, expectant, and they could both feel that for the first time in years, it began to sing.

The Parting Line

The distance appeared longer with every step. Or so it seemed to Archana. The monotony of the daily routine of walking back from work—how she hated it. Even her steps were shorn of any hurry for the destination. Like yesterday, or the day before or the uneventful days that had preceded it. She was returning home. Home from work. Work! The very word sounds like a dirge. It was nothing but a vicious life cycle. The bell, the chatter in the classroom, the hush and then the lecture or rather the straining of the voice for fifty long minutes. Then the bell would go again and a sigh of relief from the teacher and the laughter and the classroom gossip would grow louder with each step towards the staff room.

The boredom of life was writ large on her face as she paced along, arms hanging, the left resting listlessly on the leather bag that she usually carried. One could probably tell from her countenance that she was returning from some chore. And so it was! So it had been for the past year. Life seemed spent. The past to her was but a pool of memories, the future without limits, without landmarks, without hope.

Arriving home, she went to her room. The bag slipped off her shoulder onto the bed effortlessly. She felt her face with her hands and sighed. Thank God, another day was over! She picked up her towel and turned to see her mother standing at the door.

"There's a letter for you," she said.

"Leave it on the table, Mum. I shan't be long," her voice drowned behind the bathroom door.

Letter! The word almost forced itself out of her lips. There was a time, not so long ago, when this word used to inspire a special kind of tenderness, a delicacy of feeling in her heart. She had not received a letter for months now. Who would write to her? Probably, she thought, one of her students had written for some notes. How awfully boring! Back in her room, she stood wiping her face when her glance stole its way to the table. A ripple of excitement ran down her spine.

The light blue envelope with dark red and blue streaks along its edges fell with a splash on her stagnated memory. She instantly stumbled onto various fragments of her past. Her expression did not change much. She stared at it for a while, picked it up calmly, held it for a few moments, then slit the envelope open. She finished the letter in one breath and slowly re-read it again. She realized that this letter was no longer a continuation of presence but had come as an explanation of absence. This realization slightly disturbed her, only for a few moments, though. Happiness gradually percolated through her indifference.

She pulled out the disarranged drawers from the table and began combing through things. Her first endeavour did not bring her success. She was visibly annoyed. Then eventually she got half of it. A further search brought out the second half. She put the two halves together and looked down at the photograph. Didn't look the same as she remembered him. She looked into his eyes and the emotion that swelled up within her wasn't quite the same as when their eyes had met for the first time. That had been a few years ago and now all the yesterdays crowded and floated onto the surface of her consciousness. She could recall vividly his eloquent looks at the airport. The day he left for England. She remembered that his soft, dark, ardent eyes were looking at her so lovingly that she had felt in his gaze his soul searching for hers. Gazing at each other, they had silently promised to have many such moments together. No matter what happened. Somehow this feeling was no more in this photograph. Archana felt as though she was looking at his face through a cracked mirror, where indecision and confused passions fitfully flitted away.

It would have been better had she thrown away the photograph when she had torn it in a fit of anger. She had every right to be angry. He had made her believe she would be the only love he would ever have, would come back to her as soon as his studies were over. Were they all lies? Why would he stop writing otherwise? She wrote time and again. As her impatience grew, her language changed its accent from mock anger to pleading and finally to sarcasm. But to no effect. He did not write for nearly a year and Archana had stopped writing too. She felt humiliated at the thought that she would not have been the sort of girl he would have chosen had the range been wider.

And now, suddenly, here it was! She felt rather happy at not having thrown the photograph away. She got up from the bed to get the bottle of glue. While she strove to put the two pieces together, her memory made its way through the shadowy past, lifting the shroud that time had cast over her buried hopes and aspirations. How they had loved each other! How could he be so heartless? Through her entire adolescence he was the hero of her love's young dream; her entire youth she had spent in his adoration. Oh, how could it be? Why did he?

Having put the two pieces together she looked at him intently. Right through the centre of the matted black and white appeared a hairline crack that only reflected the reluctance within her. In spite of her best efforts, the photograph didn't quite look the same as before. Archana felt that the personality of the photograph somehow eluded all sense of assurance. She did not feel as much frustration as complacence. Sunil's reassuring words in the letter were not strong enough to melt away her silent apprehension that had gradually built up during the past year. The faint line of deception was almost too subtle to be ignored. It only succeeded in bringing into relief the vulnerable character of the person she once loved so dearly. She pondered over the paradox that love is a spring that enlivens our heart, yet the same heart is incapable of creating that spring. As though by revelation, Archana realized that the two pieces wouldn't fuse, shouldn't fuse, that she couldn't let them. Like a soaked blotter, the province of her heart was beyond recovery. With a misty awareness that the phantom pain would return once in a while even after the wound had healed, Archana pulled the two pieces apart for good.

The Retreat

Months whisked by without notice. Kajal returned to her father's place for the first time since marriage. She was returning from her in-laws—from the big house with a portico and a driveway to the little mofussil house, from the glamour of Calcutta to the restful Runupur, from the caresses of her loving husband to her pre-marriage existence, the uninteresting spinster's life. The unnoticed tulsi plant in the corner of the little courtyard, which used to oblige the wind in all its whims, had grown accustomed to the ways of the world. Kajal went around the house wearing the looks of a stranger. Her transformed soul was shedding a new light on her gaze. She set upon discovering the inmates with it. She felt at home for the first time in years but realized that this feeling had been alien to the environment in the past.

Beauty had not bestowed any favours on Kajal. In simple prose, she was rather unattractive. Her marriage had been a pain in the neck for her parents. Marriage proposals had followed close on the heels of advertisements in newspapers and Kajal had to sit for sweaty interviews, times without number. But all the negotiations proved no-go associations. She had to undertake short visits to Calcutta for the same reason but all turned out to be sleeveless errands. There came a time when her parents gave up all hope of her marriage and were convinced that she was destined to be on the shelf for good. In utter despair they left it to providence.

At this point of time, when conscience was hanging heavy on them, suddenly out of nowhere emerged this forty-three-year-old city dweller. He was of moderate means with a secure job and a rather large family house. He came, saw Kajal, liked her quiet ways and married her. Obliging remarks all around could draw from this man the conclusion that he was only being practical in marrying Kajal. He was of an age when looks have the glow of the setting sun and the pleasures of life have to be diluted. But snow on the rooftop doesn't always mean that there is no fire in the house. Kajal was happy. She was beside herself with joy. Her parents were relieved. Their happiness was glowing on their faces. Kajal read it immediately. She knew that she had been deprived of the warmth of their hearts since the very advent of her marriageable age. Suddenly the subject of concealed contempt had turned into a precious darling. The withered responsibility had made room for fluent discourses. They were a happy family again. The atmosphere was congenial, the air free, and Kajal began to breathe easy.

She could not help feeling surprised at her own change, though. She found it difficult to reconcile the spinster Kajal of yesterday with the housewife of today. The awful loneliness that had plagued her a few months back was not quite the same.

She felt as though she had someone to whisper to in the tranquillity of solitude and share the beauty of it. Her heart leapt up with joy. She began thinking how this heart could beat so musically, the same heart which had slept for years. There was not a stir in it then and now it was dancing delightfully. Amazing, she pondered.

Memories floated up to the surface of her consciousness. Only a few months back, she was inert mentally. She was afraid of being locked up in such loneliness that she would even stop questioning her own existence. All the girls that Kajal knew in the locality had widened their sphere of relations through marriage. Some had been lucky, some not quite. But everybody had had a chance to change their lives. With a smiling face amid the din and bustle, Kajal had waved goodbye to all of them in turn. And each time she had to swallow her strangulated sobs in solitude—not in envy for the lucky ones but in the sheer pain born out of her intimate sadness. She used to persuade herself to ignore her own being for a few days and sail with the tide of joy only to return to her awful awareness of being alone. Year after year, spring had blossomed with many a new hope but all of them had silent deaths, one after the other. Her past was but a museum of memories, and the future had no future in it.

Thus rummaging through her memories, Kajal found herself standing on the cemented ghat of their private little pond at the back of the house. She felt that her remembered sorrows were a fillip to her present happiness. This was a place she used to frequent in the past. She would come here in the dewy summer dawn, bask in the mild sunny afternoon of winter, in the twilight of many an autumn evening. She would come here for a little peace of mind. She would sit on the edge of the steps and dip her feet in the water. Sometimes she used to stir the water a bit and her reflection on the water quivered. Kajal had developed an uncanny relationship with this shadow. They used to converse for hours on end. Sometimes it would give Kajal a patient hearing, sometimes it would nod an assent within the ripples. She could not recall any bickering between the two of them. It had listened with sympathy to the vacuums, rumbles and spasms of her life, but had never shown any signs of impatience or boredom.

Kajal made herself comfortable in her old seat with a heart brimming with hope. She had stored hours of conversation all these months she had been away. It would be something quite unlike what she used to say in the past. This would be a long unbroken account of unending happiness. She had been waiting patiently for this moment to arrive.

She lifted her saree a couple of inches above her ankles and slipped her feet into the water. The trembling happiness of her soul resembled the ripples on the surface of the light green water. Kajal looked into the water but could hardly believe her eyes. Her friend started gradually drifting away with the ripples. It appeared to lose its composure. How unlike her, she thought! The reflection that would float like patience on water en rapport was growing impatient at the slightest stir. Who would listen then to the dreamy fulfilled expectations of Kajal? She had firmly believed that this watery apparition would share in her joys as it had done in her sorrows in the past.

Why had it suddenly become so self-centred? Has it spent all its energy listening to the seamy side of life alone? Despite all her efforts, she could not draw the attention of her friend. It eluded her grasp every time. It had suddenly turned into a mere shadow without depth, an imprint of a being with no dimensions. Her surprise came to a head when she found that she was not at all angry or annoyed at this show of indifference; rather, she felt a flow of gratitude through her veins. Never before had she been more close to this apparition than at this moment. She moulded a little grave with wet mud from the banks and with a pointed twig inscribed on it the words—I beg you, please forgive me.

Only to Catch an Angel

The time was twilight, dawn of night. That part of the colony had V-type two-storeyed flats. Balconies overlooked each other. Suddenly, he noticed an apparition on the opposite balcony, arms outstretched, yawning; glowing after a siesta, rain-fresh creamy skin. Her arms were rivulets of charm. She was beautiful. Beauty chiselled, bred in the bones. As their eyes met, she smiled. Teeth, a two-row necklace of pearls set between lips like plump orange cells. A faint smile slid across his face. He hadn't seen her before then. Before then meant precisely a week. A week it was since he had joined his new job.

He held his breath and let the wonder in. The idea of getting to know her was like a note struck on glass—distant yet eternal.

Opportunity knocked soon enough. He met the couple at a social gathering a few days later. A jolt of shock ran down his spine. Her husband was ugliness carved in ebony. Next to him, she looked like spilt milk on black marble. What was the missing link in the puzzle? he thought.

The puzzle was easy to solve, once he got to know them. The husband was as brilliant as the wife beautiful. Along with nature's bounty, she had brains to match, and combined, they both knew as did others around them, they were sure to go places.

He himself was as handsome as they come. Charm clung to him like second nature. The couple was the rave of the colony. Being neighbours, the three of them soon became irresistible to each other, and to others.

Time flew on the wings of good company.

That evening was like many others. Many others that had preceded it. Uneventful yet enthralling. He was having tea with her in the balcony of her flat.

A sharp shower had spring-cleaned the dusty summer afternoon. The fresh summer wind gently blew, spiced with the smell of earth. Darkness lingered on the fringes of daylight.

Conversation was casual, as usual; the atmosphere relaxed, sprinkled with laughter.

They were both waiting for her husband to return from office. "Late as usual," she put in.

Suddenly the bolt came from the blue. Unannounced, uninvited. She said she wanted to gift him a dream. Make him walk on clouds. Spacewalk, if only he agreed.

He was rooted to the sofa he sat on. A muslin awareness enveloped him and he stumbled without warning onto a moment of intimate interlude. This social situation was beyond the common run of his experience. He had no earthly idea of how to cope with it. For a moment, silence between them stood stunned in disbelief.

Gradually, composure seeped in. He heard himself say, "But I thought you loved your husband!"

"Oh! But I do. I am very much in love with him."

"Well!" incredulity throbbed again.

"You wouldn't understand . . ." she snapped, betraying no emotion.

"Give us a chance. I just might!" he sounded perhaps a trifle edgy.

"I have a promise to keep," she paused. "The heart has reasons which reason does not understand."

Bewildered, he retorted, "I don't quite get you!"

"I told you, you wouldn't."

The second cup of tea was being poured into his cup. The tinkle of spoon on fine bone china, stirring the sugar. Her gaze, weighted with purpose, melted into his eyes. And then he heard the melody whisper, words breaking on her lips like fragile bubbles.

"All for a beautiful child, you know. To catch an angel."

Walk on, Dear

"Shall we take a walk through the Maidan?" he said.

She did not reply. Just followed him.

"It's chilly this evening. Are you all right?"

"It is, isn't it?"

The Maidan was virtually empty. During winter it usually is. Save for the odd couple here and there. Perhaps trying to find a purpose for living.

They walked together. Not hand in hand, though, as they usually did. Neither of them spoke. He felt the loneliness of the Maidan gradually enveloping his soul.

"You are rather quiet today. Anything wrong in the office?" she enquired to extract words from him.

He was immersed in thought and replied after a while.

"No, no. Office is okay. Shall we sit down for some time?"

"What now? It is getting dark. No, we better walk," she said.

So they walked.

"I," he paused. "I want to tell you something. Something important . . ." He could not complete what he had intended to say. He was hesitant.

"Go on," she assured him, "I am listening."

"I am afraid . . . what I have to say . . . may hurt you."

"Oh! Then don't say it," she retorted.

"But I have to . . . you see . . . I couldn't help it." The pressure was mounting. "You know how I feel about it. I wish there was some solution. I can't stand it much longer. It had to happen . . . I mean, you knew it was coming, didn't you?" He was about to say something else.

"Stop trying to find excuses. Why don't you come out with it?" She sounded impatient.

"I am sorry, Persis. I am getting married." He forced these words through his lips.

Suddenly the walk seemed to stretch to eternity. For her. A walk to nowhere, she thought. Knowing him for the last three years became a web of insignificance. She could not think rationally. Sobs piled up in her throat. Her living ceased. Life continued. To her, he was an incurable romantic. Irresistible. Yet, from now on, she would have to resist herself. She tried hard to regain her composure. He did not say a word. She quickened her pace, as though wanting to avoid the gradually gathering darkness of the Maidan and go into the streetlights beyond.

"Do you expect me to say something? How awfully disappointed I am? Or did you think I would break down in uncontrollable tears. That's it, I know, and that's why you preferred the darkness of the secluded Maidan . . ." Her words spilled over each other as she fought back her tears.

"Try to understand, please. I beg you. Don't get angry. I have explained to you many times before. We both knew nothing would come of this association. You did, didn't you? Our backgrounds . . ."

"Oh stop talking of our backgrounds, rather your background. Doesn't it sound monotonous to your ears? Same old background every time. I am fed up of hearing it." She stopped to find her breath and stabbed in. "As if no Bengali has ever married a Parsi before."

"I shall always remember our friendship with fondness, you know that," he said meekly.

"Thank you ever so much for your kindness," words curled out of her free lips like the serpent in Eden.

"You are being sarcastic unnecessarily."

"Am I?"

"You knew I would be getting married sooner or later. I have been telling you about my parents . . ."

She didn't allow him to finish. "Don't talk like a child, Dev. You are a grown man. Why don't you admit the truth!"

"What do you mean?" he was bewildered.

"Truth, Dev. The truth. Admit it. Admit that you are a coward. You love me. I know that. You just haven't the guts to marry me. I knew it all along, only I didn't want to admit it." Her anger wanted to explode into tears. She somehow suppressed it.

There was no reply. She wasn't expecting him to reply either. There was not much left to talk about now. The future had frozen.

The main road was a few yards away. Brightly lit.

"I hope she doesn't find out," she said suddenly.

"Who?" he could not guess what she was on about.

"Your would-be wife."

"Find out what?" he was not with her at all.

They were standing on the main road. Heavy traffic.

Trying to cross the road, minding the traffic, she almost shouted, "That you are a coward."

Till We Meet Again

"Good morning. May I speak to Mr Gupta, please?"

"Good morning, sir. Who's calling, please?" the receptionist enquired.

"Bhatia. Rajen Bhatia of Bangalore."

There was a pause at the receiving end. Then the telephone receiver sprang to life.

"Hi handsome! Long time no see. Where are you speaking from?" asked Mr Gupta in an enthusiastic tone. "From the Hindustan Times building. Arrived by the morning flight. How are things with you?"

"Pretty much the same. Same routine, you know. Have you been to my place or straight airport to office?"

"I am conscientious, Tito, but I shall never be a workaholic like you. I always mix business with pleasure when time permits. Been to your place, dumped my case, had a wash and breakfast, and here I am. Actually, your charming wife is such an accomplished hostess, who can resist! Oh! By the way . . ." Rajen couldn't finish.

"Did the flight arrive on time?"

"Yes it did and thank God for that. I hate to go to the office directly from the airport. You should watch your wife you know. She is getting more beautiful each time I see her and . . ."

"How are Jaya and the kid?" enquired Tito.

"Oh, they are fine except that Jaya finds sex so very boring these days," Rajen mused.

"Serves you right, you whatnot. Anyway see you this evening, then. How long will you be in Delhi?" An unusual enquiry.

"Leaving day after tomorrow, early morning. Oh. Try to be back early from office. I shall finish by three. See you," said Rajen and hung up.

★

Gupta picked up the intercom.

"Banerjee, what time did you say the meeting was?"

"At three this afternoon, sir."

"How long do you think it will take?"

Banerjee thought for a moment.

"Couple of hours at least, sir. You know these people. They go on and on."

"See, something has come up. I was wondering, couldn't we postpone it?"

"Dare not, sir. I confirmed it only this morning. If we are not present, the case will be decided ex-parte."

"Okay, forget it. We will leave at two-thirty."

★

The phone tinkles. This time at Mr Gupta's residence in Green Park. Shalini picks it up.

"Hello?"

"Hello darling!" says a male voice at the other end.

"Oh, Rajen! Where have you been all this time? Let's see. When were you last in Delhi?" There was elation in her voice, "About six months back."

"Yes, about that," said Rajen stoically.

"When did you arrive?" she enquired.

"This morning."

"This morning! Where were you all this time! When are you coming?" impatience rang in her voice.

"I have put up in a hotel. My director is with me. It wouldn't look nice to leave him here alone and stay somewhere else," Rajen tried to reason.

"Oh but this is not the first time that he is with you. Is anything the matter?" she sounded genuinely concerned.

"You should know. Anyway, look, I will come back to you later. Have to rush now." He was nearly cutting off and then added, "How is Mukul?"

"Mukul's fine, thanks. But Rajen, may I know . . ." she couldn't finish.

"Sorry, I have to rush. Ciao for now," Rajen hung up.

Shalini appeared perplexed for a moment. She ran back the spool of her memory to find justification for Rajen's behaviour. Never before had Rajen been in Delhi without staying at their place. Possibly during the last six months, Rajen had been in Delhi and not bothered to contact them. She thought she knew the answer. Very unfortunate, she ruminated.

Till Tito's return from office that evening, there was no news of Rajen. He was surprised to learn from his wife that Rajen hadn't showed up the whole day.

"But he said he had breakfast here! I don't understand. It's funny. Why would he lie?"

"How should I know?" Shalini's voice betrayed concealed annoyance.

"Did he tell you where he was putting up?" he enquired.

"In a hotel, he said. I couldn't ask which. He wasn't on the phone long enough."

"We'll just have to wait then, I suppose. I will ring up one or two dealers he usually meets when he is here. But we shall have to wait till tomorrow anyway." There was resignation in his attitude.

That evening, Rajen didn't turn up. Nor did he ring.

Next day, Mr Gupta contacted both the dealers. They confirmed that Rajen had met them but could not enlighten

Tito as to his whereabouts in Delhi. Tito was annoyed. He suspected that he himself might be responsible. But his belief was not strong enough to allow him to wallow in his own guilt.

That evening Rajen was sitting with his friend Amit Bose in the latter's living room in Safdarjung Enclave. They were sipping whisky. The time was just past dusk.

"Weren't they annoyed? About you not staying with them?"

"Well, I told them. About time I stayed with you for a few days. It's always been them."

The TV was on. None of them was paying any attention. It was on more out of habit than interest.

"Relationships are like eels. Easy to catch but difficult to hold on to. They can be so strong, yet so brittle," Rajen said thoughtfully.

"Why this sudden burst of philosophy, I wonder!" said Amit in amusement. "Jaya doesn't appear the type you can fight with."

"Nothing wrong there, thank God."

Rajen stood up, gulped down his drink.

"May I have your car keys please?"

"Over there," said Amit, pointing to the bookcase. "Where are you off to?"

"Shan't be long. Going over to Tito's place to drop a packet I brought from Bangalore."

He picked up the keys from the top of the bookcase and saw himself out.

Amit concentrated on the TV. Poured himself another drink, lit a cigarette and made himself comfortable on the sofa. The programme changed. A ghazal singer came on. He had a rich mellow voice. Amit was immersed in it. His concentration was suddenly broken by the ringing of the doorbell.

He got up and opened the front door to find Rajen waiting.

"Back so early?" enquired Amit.

"They aren't in. Typical of Delhi. Don't have full-time domestic helps. I kept on ringing their bell. No one opened."

"Never mind. Just as well. Had they been in, you wouldn't be back before midnight," said Amit happily.

"Do me a favour, Amit. Drop this packet at their flat tomorrow. Won't be too far out of your way back from office," said Rajen and handed over the packet to Amit.

"Same place, isn't it, 2nd floor? On the right of the landing. I forget the number of the flat."

"Yes, you are right. Flat no. 6."

★

That evening, more drinks were consumed than usual. Rajen was in a philosophical mood throughout. He had gone on about human sensitivity, stupid misunderstandings.

He had concluded that faith was disappearing fast from behavioural interactions. Amit had been a patient listener.

Rajen Bhatia left for Bangalore the morning after, as scheduled.

★

That evening, Amit called on the Guptas. The couple answered the door almost together. Seeing him, their faces lit up. They were sure Rajen would be with him. But by that time, Rajen was in Bangalore.

"Where's Rajen?" both of them enquired almost simultaneously.

"Rajen?" Amit was puzzled. "Didn't you know he was leaving this morning?"

"I think he did mention he would," said Mr Gupta.

Amit handed the packet over to Shalini.

"This is for you. Rajen asked me to hand it over to you."

"Do sit down. You have come after a long time," implored Shalini.

"Not today, sorry. Some other time, perhaps. Someone will be calling on me this evening." Amit was preparing to leave.

Shalini and Tito were both itching to ask why Rajen could not come over himself to hand over the packet. They didn't have to wait long for the answer.

"Actually, it's unfortunate that you weren't in last evening. Otherwise . . ." Amit couldn't finish.

"Who wasn't in last evening?" said Tito.

"You had gone out somewhere last evening, hadn't you?" Now it was Amit's turn to be surprised.

"Both of us were in. In fact, we were waiting for Rajen till about tea. We had our dinner after that," Shalini added, wanting to get to the bottom of the mystery.

"Sorry, I don't understand. Rajen had come yesterday. At least that's what he told me. He said he rang the bell and no one answered. Anyway, I think there's some mistake somewhere. Sorry, I can't stay any longer. See you." Amit went out.

Tito and Shalini stood silent, looking at each other. The happenings of the last twenty-four hours had been strange, to say the least. Tito regained his poise after some time and closed the door of the flat.

"I am not sure what to make of this," said Tito.

Shalini did not reply.

She opened the neatly bound parcel. Out came three small packets. A tin box containing Cadbury's chocolates with a little card stuck to it. On it was written, "To Mukul, with love from Uncle." The second one was a box of Mysore *paak* with another card stuck on top. "To Shalini, from Rajen Bhatia."

Shalini handed over the third small packet to Tito. It was a paper carton containing three cakes of export-quality sandalwood soap with a small envelope marked

"Tito. Confidential." Tito was confused. Curious too. He tore the envelope open and took out the small note. Just a couple of lines were handwritten on it, signed by Rajen.

It read: "These are the best of their kind available in India. It is meant to clean the flesh, not the spirit. But it just might. Give it a try anyway."

Tito walked up to the window, note in hand.

"What has he written?" enquired Shalini, hoping that it contained the clue that would solve the mystery.

"Nothing much. One of his usual saucy jokes," said Tito, tearing the note to tiny pieces.

He turned to face his wife and said thoughtfully, "I think it's about time we paid a visit to Bangalore."

About the Author

B huban Basu is a chartered accountant from England and Wales and has forty-six years of experience in the field. Literature has always been more than a hobby and his writings, both fiction and non-fiction, have appeared in leading newspapers such as *The Times of India*, *The Telegraph* and *The Statesman*. He lives in Kolkata with his family.